# HERGÉ

# THE ADVENTURES OF TINTIN

# TINTIN IN AMERICA

Translated by Leslie Lonsdale-Cooper
and Michael Turner

Artwork copyright © 1945 by Éditions Casterman, Tournai.
Copyright © renewed 1973 by Casterman.
Library of Congress Catalogue Card Numbers Afor 1107 and R 558598
Text © 1978 by Egmont Children's Books Ltd.
First published in Great Britain in 1978.
Magnet edition first published in 1979 by Methuen Children's Books Ltd.
Reprinted nine times
Reissued 1989 by Mammoth,
an imprint of Egmont Children's Books Limited
239 Kensington High Street, London W8 6SL

Reprinted 1990, 1992, 1993 (twice), 1994, 1995 (twice), 1996, 1997, 1998.

Printed by Casterman, S.A., Tournai, Belgium.
ISBN 0-7497-0230-3

# TINTIN
## IN
## AMERICA

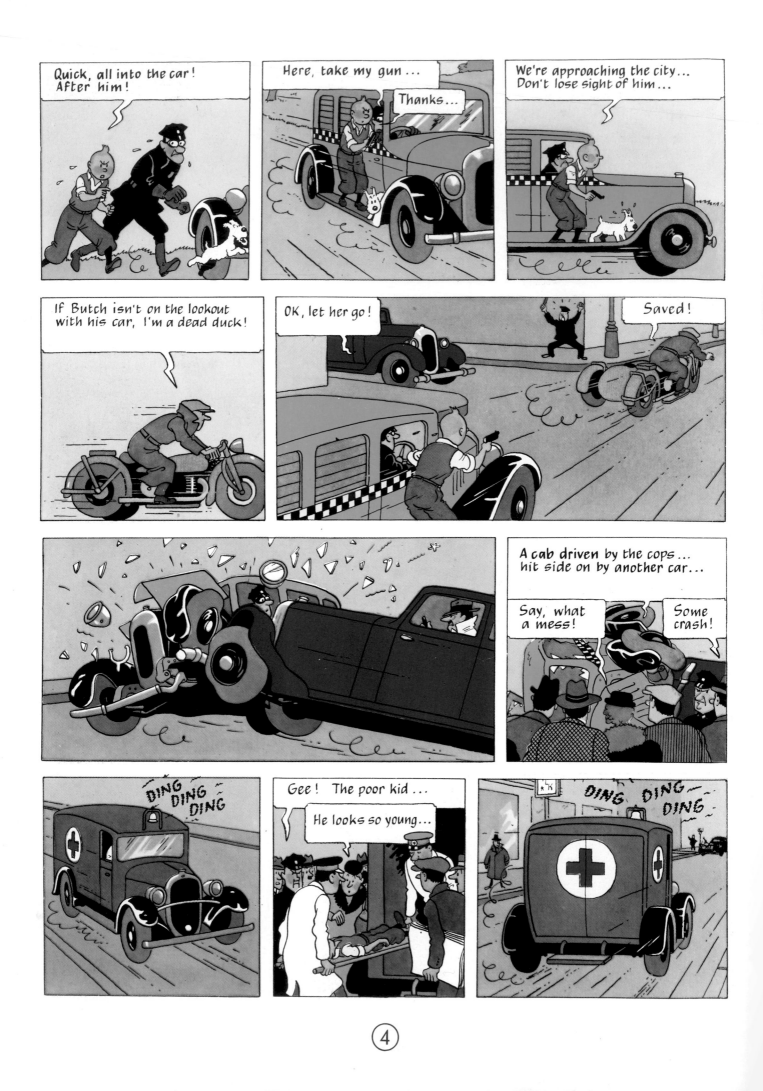

Some days later...

HOSP

I'm glad to be back on my feet again. It could have been much worse...

Fresh air at last! I feel better already!

Rush hour!

What does a dog do in Chicago when he wants to cross?

CLACK

No one's noticed me...

That's that then... Tell the boss, will you?

Take it easy, bambino, I gotta you covered. The boss... he's-a coming...

W-w-what... h-h-happened?...

So! The famous reporter!... A little kid with big ideas, like he's gonna make war on Al Capone... On me, the King of Chicago!

You done a good job. Here's the dough.

Thanks, boss.

And that's for you. Now, just get that little squirt out of my hair, permanently!

Sure, boss.

Holy smoke!... A real little tough guy!... He knocked out the boss, and Pietro too!

Good, he's gone!... I must take care of the other two before he comes back...

Whoops! There's one...

...and now the other... Both securely tied... The third man will be along soon ... Ah, I can hear him... he's coming back...

Where the heck can he be hiding?

Watch it, Tintin, he's coming...

That puts paid to gangster number three. Now for the police...

Game, set and match!

Quick, officer, I've just caught Al Capone himself and two of his gangsters!

Sarge?... Send a car along. I just picked up a nutcase...thinks he captured Al Capone and a couple of his hoods.

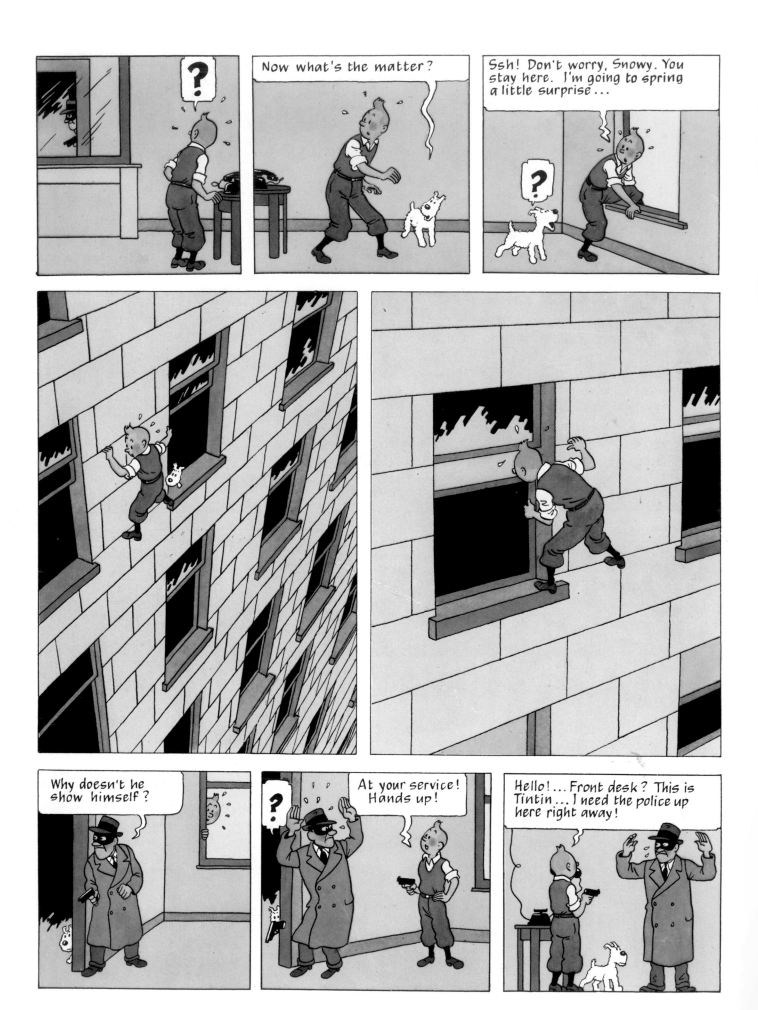

Ha! ha! ha! That'll teach you to play cowboys! By the time he's managed to untangle himself I'll be far away!

Sing Sing!... Redskins! How do I talk myself out of this one?

How! Mighty Sachem, I come in peace!

How, Paleface! What brings white man to hunting grounds of Blackfeet?

Mighty Sachem, I come to warn you. A young white warrior is riding this way. His heart is full of hate and his tongue is forked! Beware of him, for he seeks to steal the hunting grounds of the noble Blackfeet. I have spoken!...

Hear me, brave Blackfeet! A young Paleface approaches. He seeks, by trickery, to steal our hunting grounds!... May Great Manitou fill our hearts with hate and strengthen our arms!... Let us raise the tomahawk against this miserable Paleface with the heart of a prairie dog!

As for Paleface-with-eyes-of-the-Moon, he has warned us of danger that hangs over our heads, and will soon come upon Blackfeet. May Great Manitou heap blessings upon him!

Now let us raise the tomahawk...

Big Chief him say well...

Pipe of peace! I can't remember where in the world we buried the hatchet when we finished our last bit of fighting...

Heck!

Hello, here come the Indians... I tell you Snowy, if I didn't know the redskins are peaceful nowadays, I'd be feeling a lot less sure of myself!

Well, I'm scared to death!

What's all this?... It's an odd sort of way to welcome a stranger!

Whew! They've gone! Savages! Frightened me out of my wits!

Snowy, that was disgraceful! You abandoned Tintin.

Really, what curious customs you have!

Truly, Paleface does not have stomach of a squaw. He smiles and is calm.

But we see what he does later!

Face it Snowy... You've got a yellow streak. For all you know, Tintin's in danger...

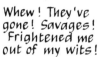 

Hear, O Paleface, the words of Great Sachem...You have come among Blackfoot people with heart full of trickery and hate, like a sneaking dog. But now you are tied to torture stake. You shall pay Blackfeet for your treachery by suffering long. I have spoken!

What sort of talk is that?

Now, let my young braves practise their skills upon this Paleface with his soul of a coyote! Make him suffer long before you send him to land of his forefathers!

But...he's crazy!

You speak well, O Sachem!

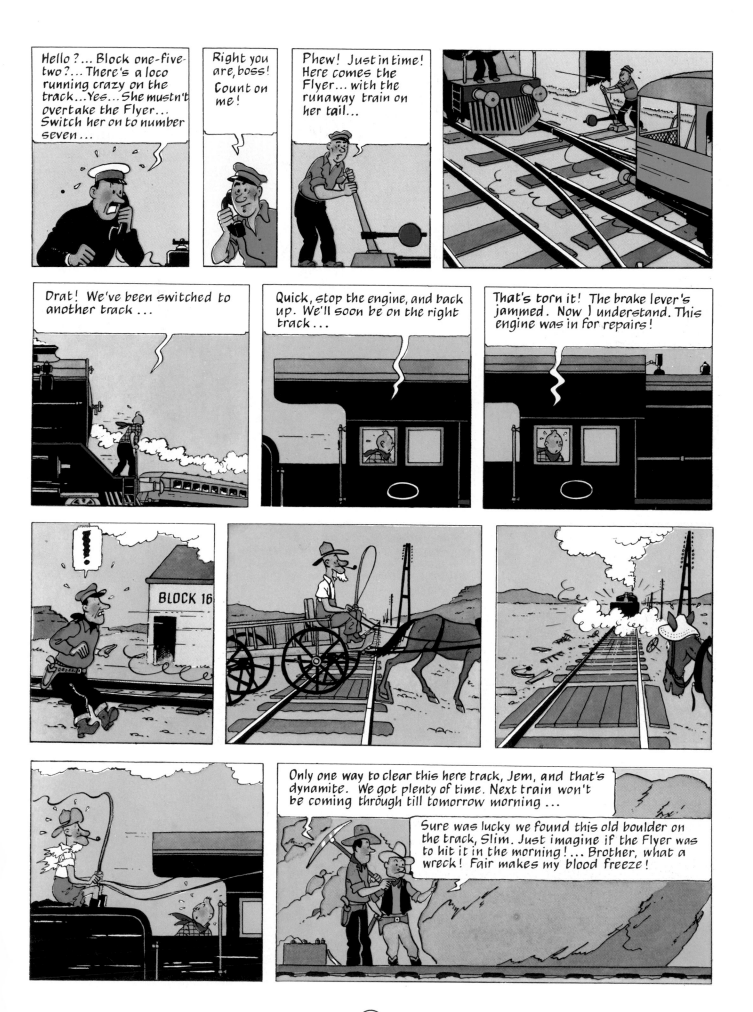

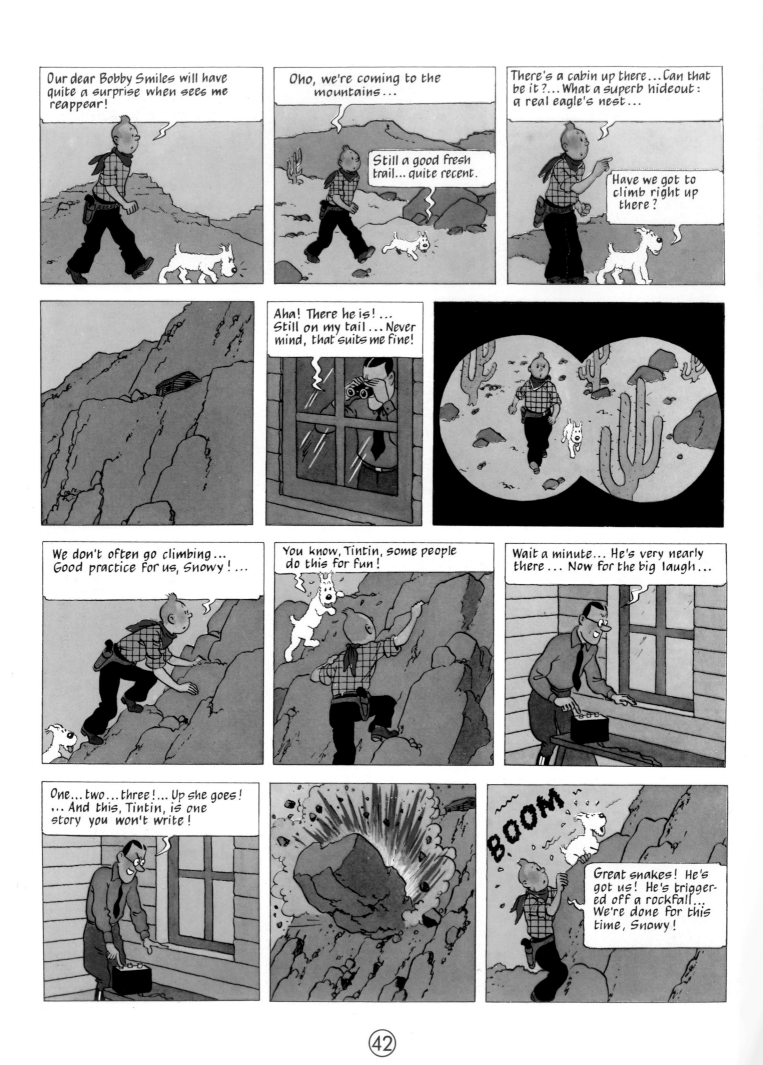

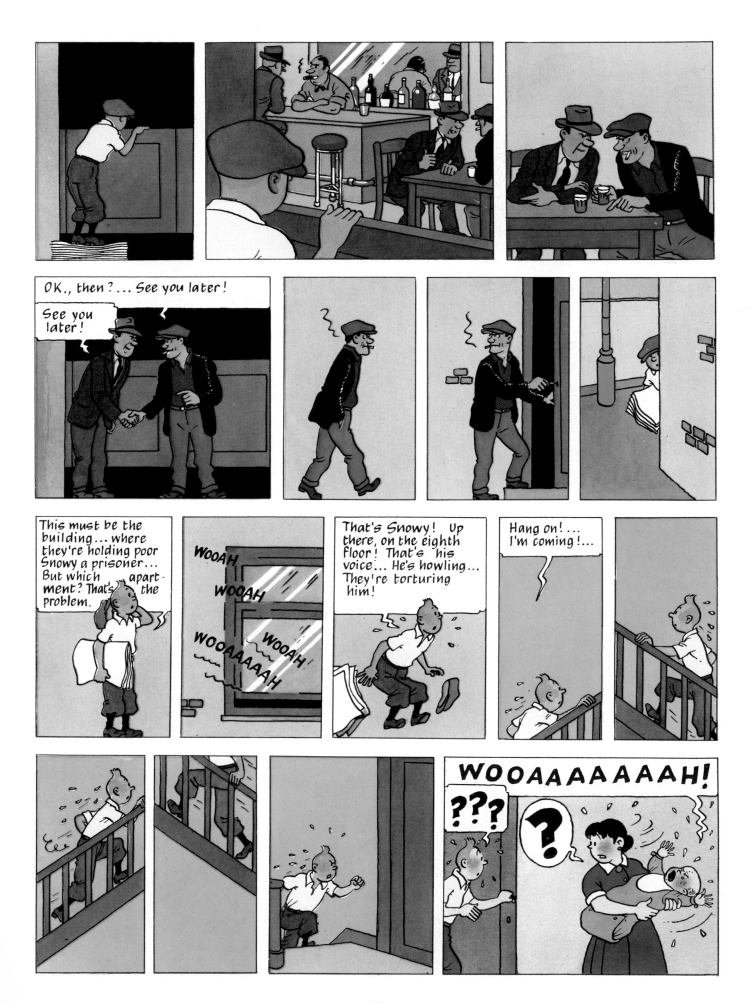

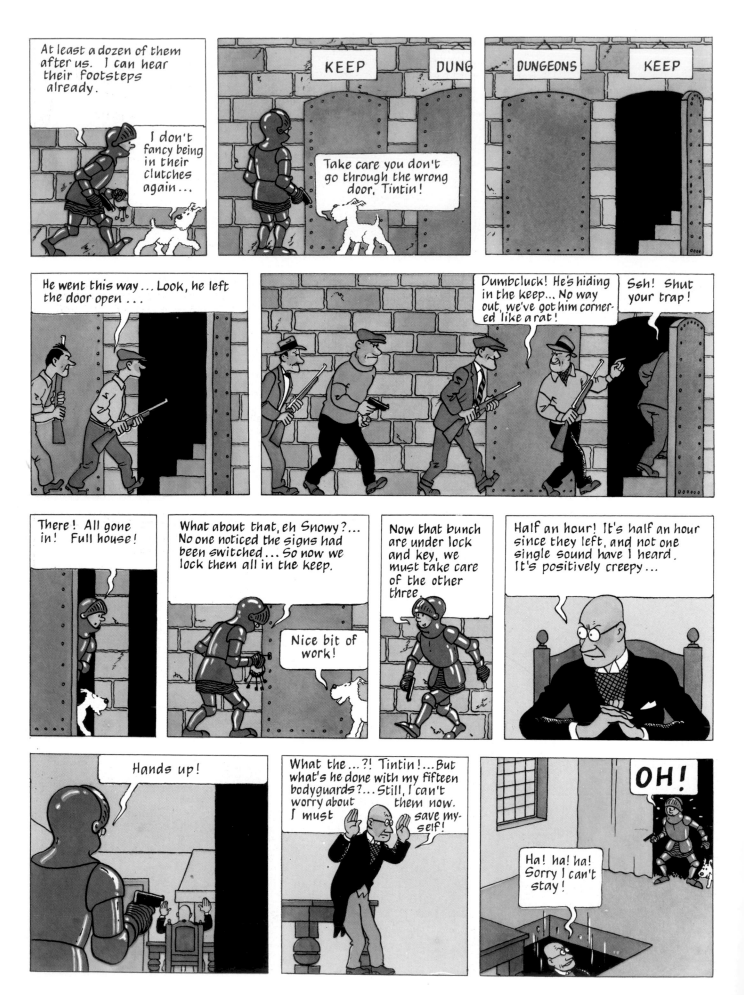

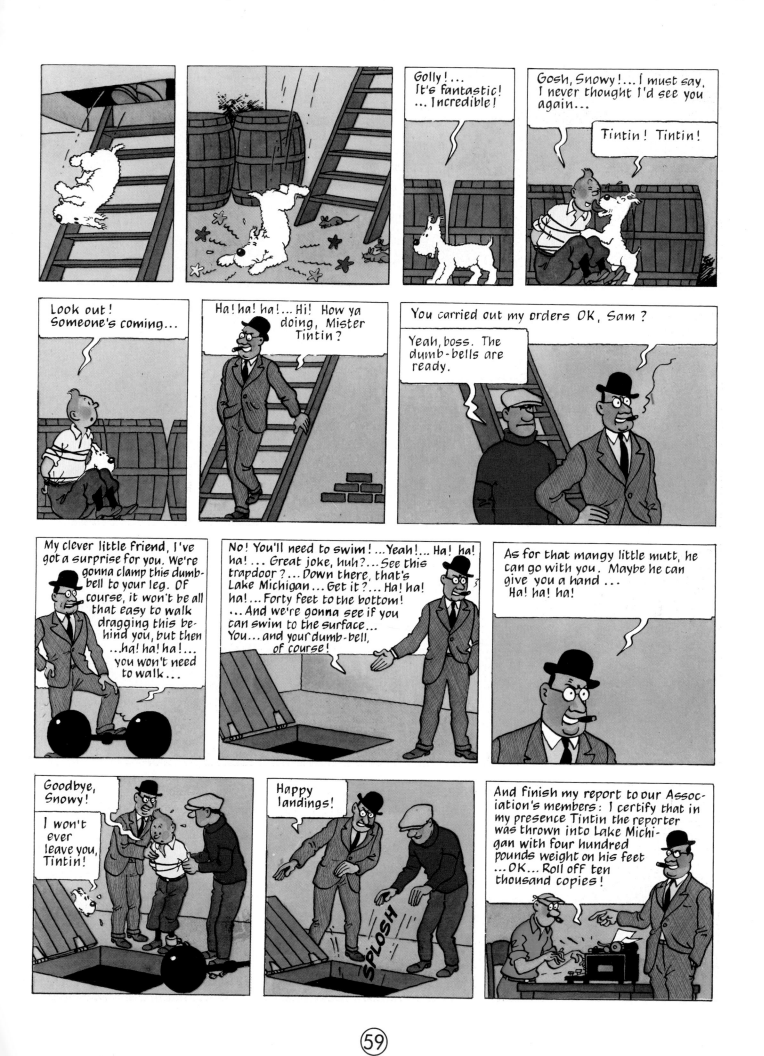

Sensational developments in the Tintin story!...
The famous and friendly reporter re-appears! Tintin, missing some days back from a banquet in his honour, led police to the hideout of the Central Syndicate of Chicago Gangsters. Apprehended were 355 suspects, and police collected hundreds of documents, expected to lead to many more arrests... This is a major clean-up for the city of Chicago... Mr Tintin admitted that the gangsters had been ruthless enemies, cruel and desperate men. More than once he nearly lost his life in the heat of his fight against crime... Today is his day of glory. We know that every American will wish to show his gratitude, and honour Tintin the reporter and his faithful companion Snowy, heroes who put out of action the bosses of Chicago's underworld!

LONG LIVE TINTIN & SNOWY

After a full round of celebrations, Tintin and Snowy embark for Europe...

Pity!... I was almost beginning to get used to it!

TOOOOOT

HERGÉ